WE LOVE FISHING!

written by Ariel Bernstein   illustrated by Marc Rosenthal

A Paula Wiseman Book · Simon & Schuster Books for Young Readers
New York London Toronto Sydney New Delhi

SIMON & SCHUSTER BOOKS FOR YOUNG READERS
An imprint of Simon & Schuster Children's Publishing Division
1230 Avenue of the Americas, New York, New York 10020
Text copyright © 2021 by Ariel Bernstein Books LLC
Illustrations copyright © 2021 by Marc Rosenthal
SIMON & SCHUSTER BOOKS FOR YOUNG READERS
is a trademark of Simon & Schuster, Inc.
For information about special discounts for bulk purchases, please contact
Simon & Schuster Special Sales at 1-866-506-1949 or business@simonandschuster.com.
The Simon & Schuster Speakers Bureau can bring authors to your live event.
For more information or to book an event, contact the Simon & Schuster Speakers Bureau at
1-866-248-3049 or visit our website at www.simonspeakers.com.
Book design by Lizzy Bromley
The text for this book was set in Adobe Caslon.
The illustrations for this book were rendered in Prismacolor pencil and digital color.
Manufactured in China
1120 SCP
First Edition
2 4 6 8 10 9 7 5 3 1
CIP data for this book is available from the Library of Congress.
ISBN 978-1-5344-3864-4
ISBN 978-1-5344-3865-1 (eBook)

For Ali Bovis, Emma Bland Smith,
Katey Howes, and Kristin Mahoney
—A. B.

For my father-in-law, Jack,
who loved fishing
—M. R.

Bear, Porcupine, Otter, and Squirrel love fishing.

I love fishing.

I love fishing.

They love fishing.

Bear, Porcupine, Otter, and Squirrel can't wait to eat lots of fish.

I'll skewer my fish for a shish kebab.

I'll eat mine after dessert!

Fish smell
too fishy.

Bear, Porcupine, Otter, and Squirrel love to walk through the woods on their way to fish.

Bear, Porcupine, Otter, and Squirrel love to sit in their boat for hours as they fish.

Bear, Porcupine, Otter, and Squirrel love fishing so much, they don't even mind when it rains.

I needed a shower anyway.

Rain makes my fur frizz.

Bear, Porcupine, Otter, and Squirrel think they feel a pull on the rod.

Bear, Porcupine, Otter, and Squirrel are excited about their catch.

I don't want to hold it!

Why's it looking at me? It smells kinda fishy.

It's so slippery!

Hey, where's it going?

Oops.

Bear, Porcupine, Otter, and Squirrel could always try to catch another fish.

Bear, Porcupine, Otter, and Squirrel
are done fishing for the day.
They do not always love fishing.

Where's the nearest restaurant?

Two miles. More exercise.

I'm going to need dessert.

But everyone loves Squirrel.

Especially Fish.